For Dad, much love.

LONDON BOROUGH OF WANDSWORTH	
9030 00004 3108 5	
Askews & Holts	18-Jun-2015
JF	£10.99
	WW15001938

Bloomsbury Publishing, London, New Delhi, New York and Sydney

First published in Great Britain in 2015 by Bloomsbury Publishing Plc
50 Bedford Square, London, WC1B 3DP

Text and illustrations copyright © Tom McLaughlin 2015
The moral right of the author/illustrator has been asserted

A CIP catalogue record for this book is available from the British Library

ISBN 978 1 4088 5496 9

Printed in China by Leo Paper Products, Heshan, Guangdong

1 3 5 7 9 10 8 6 4 2

www.bloomsbury.com

All papers used by Bloomsbury Publishing are natural, recyclable products
made from wood grown in well-managed forests.
The manufacturing processes conform to the environmental regulations of the country of origin

BLOOMSBURY is a registered trademark of Bloomsbury Publishing Plc

The Cloudspotter

Tom McLaughlin

BLOOMSBURY

LONDON   NEW DELHI   NEW YORK   SYDNEY

His real name was Franklin.
But everyone called him The Cloudspotter.

The Cloudspotter didn't have many friends.
It was just him and his clouds, always.

He would spend his days,
all by himself,
spotting...

big clouds,

squeaky clouds,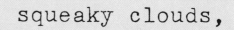

sneaky
pretend-they-can't-see-you
clouds

and angry clouds.

You see, The Cloudspotter
didn't just spot clouds.
He spotted adventures in the sky.

That way, he didn't
feel so alone.

He could swim with
giant jellyfish,

drive racing cars,

and be the KING OF THE CASTLE.

But one day everything changed.
The Scruffy Dog came along.

And she seemed to be
looking for something, too.

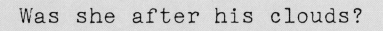

Was she after his clouds?

The Cloudspotter wasn't happy.
He wasn't used to sharing his clouds with anyone.

But The Scruffy Dog didn't seem to care.

Wherever The Cloudspotter went,
that bothersome dog went too...

...no matter what
time of day...

or night!

Before long, she was even playing
along in his adventures.

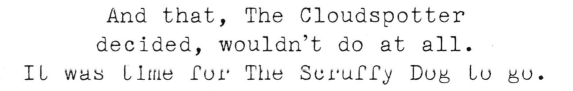

And that, The Cloudspotter
decided, wouldn't do at all.
It was time for The Scruffy Dog to go.

The Cloudspotter put
his plan into action...

...and, at last, he was alone again.

He should have been happy.
He should have been pleased.

However, something just didn't feel right.
The Cloudspotter was LONELY.

Could it be, he wondered, that The Scruffy Dog
had been searching for something else?

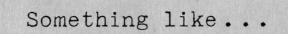

Something like . . .

a friend!

Because, everyone knows,
TWO cloudspotters are better than one...

especially when you are
BEST FRIENDS!